ACTS OF GOD

Other titles by Andy Back:

Dan the Man: The Storyline
101 Dynamic Ideas for Your Youth Group

Author's Note

The Storyline Series is intended for use by teenagers who might otherwise not read the Bible. It is by no means a replacement for, or a commentary on, the books but is a way of putting over the drama of the stories.

I have been determined throughout to remain true to the Bible, which I honour and respect as the inspired Word of God. My experience, gained over many years, is that young people may be reluctant to read the Bible, put off by old-fashioned or difficult language, as well as by such practical considerations as the size of print and the sheer volume of material.

The idea of this book is to whet your appetite, so that you will be more confident to dig into the Bible for yourself, discovering that it is not as daunting as you may have imagined. At the very least, you will be familiar with the story and the themes which will be covered.

Andy Back

ACTS OF GOD

Andy Back

Storyline Series

WORD PUBLISHING
Word (UK) Ltd
Milton Keynes, England
WORD AUSTRALIA
Kilsyth, Victoria, Australia
WORD COMMUNICATIONS LTD
Vancouver, B.C., Canada
STRUIK CHRISTIAN BOOKS (PTY) LTD
Maitland, South Africa
ALBY COMMERCIAL ENTERPRISES PTE LTD
Balmoral Road, Singapore
CHRISTIAN MARKETING NEW ZEALAND LTD
Havelock North, New Zealand
JENSCO LTD
Hong Kong
SALVATION BOOK CENTRE
Malaysia

ACTS OF GOD: THE STORYLINE
©1991 Andy Back
Published in the UK by Word (UK) Ltd. / Frontier Publishing International.

All rights reserved.

No part of this publication may be reproduced or transmitted in any form or by any means, electronic or mechanical, including photocopy, recording or any information storage or retrieval system, without permission in writing from the publishers.

ISBN 0-85009-701-0 (Australia ISBN 1-86258-165-7)

Illustrated by **Ivan Hissey**

Frontier Publishing International is committed to the production of printed and recorded materials with the view to reaching this generation with the gospel of the kingdom. FPI is part of New Frontiers International, a team ministry led by Terry Virgo, which is involved in planting and equipping churches according to New Testament principles. New Frontiers International is also responsible for a wide range of training programmes and conferences.

Reproduced, printed and bound in Great Britain for Word (UK) Ltd. by Cox & Wyman Ltd., Reading, Berks

91 92 93 94 / 10 9 8 7 6 5 4 3 2 1

Contents

	Preface	9
Part One	(Acts 1:1–2:47) From Jesus and the Eleven to the Three Thousand and Twelve	11
Part Two	(Acts 3:1–5:42) A Lame Man Stands Up and the Council Get Wound Up	14
Part Three	(Acts 6:1–8:3) The Seven, Stephen, the Stoning and Saul	18
Part Four	(Acts 8:4–9:31) A Crusade, a Conversion, and a Complete Change of Heart	20
Part Five	(Acts 9:32–12:25) The First Gentile Christian and the World's Worst Prayer Meeting	24
Part Six	(Acts 13:1–15:35) Troublesome Towns, Dodgy Discipleship and Godly Guidelines	28

Part Seven	*(Acts 15:36–18:28)* **A Change of Teams, a Change of Heart and a Change of Haircut**	34
Part Eight	*(Acts 19:1–21:32)* **Trouble in Ephesus, and Big Trouble in Jerusalem**	41
Part Nine	*(Acts 21:33–26:32)* **Paul Gives Three Sermons, Survives Two Plots and Wins One Trip to Rome**	46
Part Ten	*(Acts 27:1–28:31)* **A Storm, a Sandbank, a Shipwreck and a Snake**	51
	Glossary	57

For
Mike Sprenger,
whose series of Bible studies
brought to life
the Book of Acts for me

Preface

There is great drama in the Acts of the Apostles. I have no doubt that this remarkable story of missionary endeavour, church planting, evangelism, discipleship and commitment to the Lord, whatever the cost, has important messages for us as Christians in the latter part of the twentieth century.

The Church of today must maintain the pioneering attitude described in this biblical book. There are still countries to reach with the good news, and there are many sub-cultures within what are largely regarded as "Christian" nations which need to hear the gospel.

This book is not supposed to be an exact translation from the Greek (I know a little Greek; he runs a Kebab shop on Queen's Road – ha), but a re-working of the text, so that it's easier to understand. It gives you an idea of the story so that when you read the Bible you will have a clearer picture of what is happening.

My prayer is that every reader will determine to become like Peter, Philip, Apollos and Paul, risking everything for the sake of the Lord who gave everything for us, experiencing the mighty power of the Holy Spirit and His gifts, and spreading the good news with boldness.

APB, Brighton, July 1991

Part One
(Acts 1:1–2:47)
From Jesus and the Eleven to the Three Thousand and Twelve

The story kicks off with Luke's introduction, reminding his readers that this follows on directly from Luke's Gospel.

Jesus appeared to the disciples many times after His resurrection.

The disciples were told by Jesus to wait in Jerusalem until the Holy Spirit came upon them. Jesus ascended to heaven, and promised that He would return in exactly the same way.

The apostles (as they were known from that time) returned to Jerusalem as instructed.

Peter spoke to them about Judas, who betrayed Jesus. Judas used the money he had been paid for his crime to buy a field, but he fell to his death in the field

– all his innards spilled out, and the place is known as "The Field of Blood".

So the apostles drew lots to decide who should replace Judas as one of the apostles, and someone called Matthias was chosen. We never hear anything else about him, ever.

It came around to the time of the Jewish festival of Pentecost, and all the believers were gathered in one place.

The Holy Spirit entered the room where they were, and they were all filled and spoke in other languages, as the Spirit enabled them. They made a colossal din, and a crowd of Jews gathered.

They each heard the believers in their own language, and some thought the men were drunk.

Peter then stood up and preached an amazing sermon about the history of the Jews and about Jesus, God's Son, who died and rose again. At the end of the sermon, the people asked, "What shall we do?" Peter told them to repent and be baptised in water, and about 3000 became believers that day.

Life in the early Church consisted of meeting to hear the preaching, to break bread together, to share fellowship and to pray.

Acts 1:1–2:47

Many miracles were done through the apostles, and the believers shared their property with one another.

And even more people became believers every day.

Part Two
(Acts 3:1–5:42)
A Lame Man Stands Up and the Council Get Wound Up

Peter and John go to the Temple and find a man of forty with a serious leg problem – the problem was that his legs had never been strong enough to support his body. The man was healed in the name of Jesus Christ of Nazareth. He leapt up and ran into the Temple to praise God.

The crowds were astonished, and Peter preached another of his amazing sermons. Before he could finish, a posse of guards, priests and Sadducees barged in and arrested Peter and John. They were thrown into prison overnight.

Peter and John were tried the next morning, and they were asked by what power they were able to do the healing stuff. Peter was full of the Holy Spirit and... you guessed it, preached another of his amazing sermons. The members of the council couldn't deny that a miracle had happened. In the end, the judges

Acts 3:1–5:42

told Peter to be quiet about Jesus and to give up preaching. He replied, "We cannot stop speaking of what we have seen and heard."

The apostles were warned and released. Peter and John legged it back to the rest of the apostles and told them what had happened. They prayed together for boldness, and asked God to continue to perform miracles through them.

When they finished praying, the room was shaken by the power of the Lord and the apostles proclaimed the good news with great boldness.

Acts of God

The believers lived without disputing who owned what, and shared everything. People would sell what they owned, and the money would be distributed according to people's needs.

However, a couple named Ananias and Sapphira told a lie to Peter about what they were giving. They didn't live to regret it, since God struck them both dead. God takes lies very seriously.

The apostles performed many more mighty miracles, and the Church continued to grow as people were added to their number. They had impact throughout Jerusalem and in other nearby towns.

The religious leaders became jealous of this, so they arrested the apostles and threw them in the public jail. But God had other plans, and an angel came during the night and let them all out. By dawn, the apostles were in the Temple again, proclaiming the good news about Jesus.

The council meanwhile sent to the prison for the apostles, but they were no longer there! They then sent guards to the Temple to pull the apostles in again. "We gave you strict orders, and you just disobey us!" they said to the apostles. Peter said, "We must obey God."

The council got wild this time, and wanted to have the apostles executed. But one of them spoke sense for a change and they decided to whip the apostles and let them go, ordering them never to speak of Jesus again – some chance! The apostles went straight back to the Temple to proclaim the message of the good news to the people.

Part Three
(Acts 6:1–8:3)
The Seven, Stephen, the Stoning and Saul

The Church kept on growing, and some hassle started about some of the foreign widows missing out on the food distribution. So the apostles decided that seven men should be appointed to serve the people, to leave those with preaching gifts to get on with their job.

Everyone thought this a great move, and seven were chosen, including Stephen - more about him in the paragraph after next.

The word continued to spread, and even many priests accepted the faith.

Stephen was a man full of grace and power, and he performed many miracles among the crowds. He was opposed by some Jews, and they bribed some men to tell lies about him. He was arrested and taken before the council.

Acts 6:1–8:3

Stephen was given the opportunity, so he preached a long and involved sermon, all about Abraham and Moses. The council members got angry, but Stephen saw a vision of Jesus at the right hand of God.

He was attacked by the council, who took him out of the city and, after handing their coats to a young man named Saul to look after them (and a lot more of him later), they threw rocks at Stephen until he died.

The Church then went through a time of persecution (and more of this later, too) and the believers had to leave Jerusalem to get away from the opposition. The apostles stayed, however.

The young man Saul became active in arresting believers everywhere.

Part Four
(Acts 8:4–9:31)
A Crusade, a Conversion and a Complete Change of Heart

One of the apostles, Philip, was having a tent crusade in a local city. People saw God perform many miracles through him.

A magician by the name of Simon who had previously been very famous in that town became a believer, and he was baptised in water. He was astonished to see the amazing things God did through Phil.

Reports of this crusade got back to the apostles in Jerusalem, and they sent Peter and John to check it out. When they got there, they began to pray for people to be baptised with the Holy Spirit.

Simon the ex-magician saw this happening and thought he'd have a piece of the action. He offered Peter some cash, asking him to give him the power to be able to pray for people to be baptised with the Spirit.

Acts 8:4–9:31

He had not just misunderstood, but he thought he could buy God's gift. Peter was angry, and told Simon to repent. Simon did. Soon afterwards, Peter and John went back to Jerusalem, preaching as they went.

Philip, meanwhile, was told to go to the desert. It so happened that a man from Ethiopia in Africa was riding along the road when Phil arrived. The man was reading aloud from Isaiah.

Phil asked him if he understood what he was reading about the lamb being sacrificed. He said, "No" in his deep Ethiopian voice. Philip got into his chariot and explained the good news of Jesus to him.

He was baptised straight away in an oasis. When they came up out of the water, the Holy Spirit took Phil away.

Acts of God

While all this was happening to Philip, Saul was hard at work trying to round up the believers and put them in prison.

He was on his way to Damascus (he had heard there were quite a few believers there), when suddenly God broke into his life. He was blinded by a light, and instructed to meet a man named Ananias (not the one who had died, but another guy of the same name).

God also spoke to Ananias, who wasn't too pleased, since he'd heard of Saul and his hatred of the believers. But he obeyed God and Saul was baptised with the Spirit and in water.

Saul began to preach about Jesus straight away, which amazed everyone who thought he was opposed to the gospel.

Acts 8:4–9:31

Eventually, the Jews were so fed up with all this that they plotted to kill Saul, but he made his getaway in a basket (he was lowered out of a hole in the city wall, so that he didn't have to use the gates, which were being staked out).

Saul went to Jerusalem, where he got a not very warm welcome from the believers, because they were afraid he was only pretending to believe. But Barnabas came to Saul's help and showed the others that he was worthy of their trust. It wasn't long before the Jews in Jerusalem were out for Saul's blood, once he started preaching, so the apostles sent him off to another town.

A short time of peace followed, and the Church grew in strength, as the Holy Spirit ministered to them.

Part Five
(Acts 9:32–12:25)
The First Gentile Christian and the World's Worst Prayer Meeting

Peter was preaching the word and God used him to heal a man who had been paralysed for eight years.

In another town he came across a load of people who told him about a good woman named Dorcas who had died. He went to where her body was and she was miraculously raised from the dead!

Peter stayed in this town with a man named Simon the Tanner.

There was a Gentile named Cornelius who had a vision, and an angel told him to go and find Peter. He sent his servants to seek him out.

While they were on their way, God spoke to Peter in a vision of a sheet filled with animals, and showed him that Gentiles were welcome as believers too, not just converted Jews. Cornelius' servants turned up, and Peter went with them. When Peter arrived, Cornelius explained about his vision.

Peter preached what was for him a very short but totally amazing sermon, and everyone in the house gets saved! They also speak with other tongues, as a sign of them being baptised in the Spirit. So Peter thinks to himself, "Why not?" and they are all baptised in water too!

This seemed a bit out of order to some of the apostles, so they all got together in Jerusalem to sort it out.

Peter told them what had happened. God had done everything – all he did was obey God! When they heard this, they stopped their criticising and rejoiced, "God has given the Gentiles the opportunity to repent, too!"

There were believers preaching all over the region, and many people were saved. News of these successes reached the apostles, who sent Barnabas (the one who had believed in Saul from the start) to Antioch, where he was joined by Saul. For a year they stayed there, teaching. It was here that believers were first called "Christians".

A prophet declared there was to be a famine, and so the church in Antioch sent Saul and Barnabas to Judea with some money to help the Christians there.

Acts of God

King Herod began to persecute the Church. He had James (John's brother) killed by the sword, and then he arrested Peter.

The people of the church were praying for him, when an angel rescued Peter. He went to the house where the Christians were praying and had to knock several times before they believed it was him and that their prayers had been answered!

Next morning, the guards who had been watching over Peter were put to death by King Herod, who was furious. He became more and more unrighteous, and in the end paraded himself as a god before the people. He did not repent of this, and he died, eaten up from the inside by worms.

The word of God continued to spread and Barnabas and Saul, with a man named John Mark, returned from Jerusalem to Antioch.

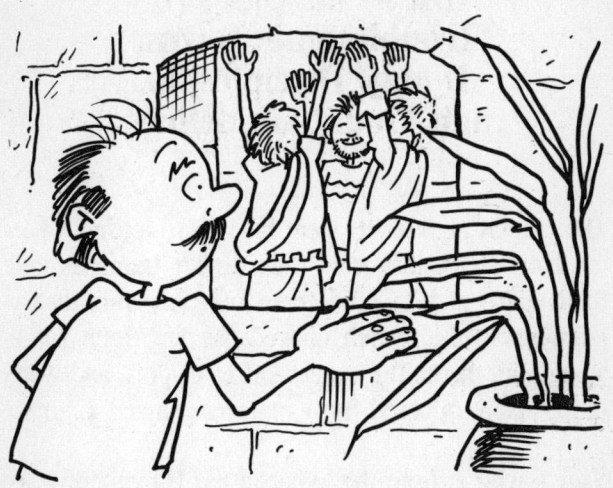

Part Six
(Acts 13:1–15:35)
Troublesome Towns, Dodgy Discipleship and Godly Guidelines

The church at Antioch were having a meeting when the Holy Spirit instructed them to set Barnabas and Saul apart, and to send them off on a missionary journey. So the church obeyed, sending John Mark along with them. They sailed off to Cyprus, and were immediately opposed by a magician named Elymas.

Saul – who is from this point in the Bible known as Paul – said to him, "You are full of evil tricks – the Lord will strike you blind for a while!" And for a while Elymas was blinded.

The town governor saw what had happened, and he was well impressed.

Paul and the others sailed on to Pamphylia, where John Mark left them and went home to Jerusalem. Paul and Barnabas went into a synagogue one Sabbath

Acts 13:1–15:35

Acts of God

and Paul was invited to speak, as was the custom. Paul didn't need to be asked twice! He preached an amazing sermon about King David and Jesus. It was so good, he was invited back again next week! And that time, nearly the whole town was there to hear what he had to say.

The Jewish authorities became jealous and disputed Paul's teaching. But Paul spoke out boldly, and many were saved. Then Paul and Barnabas were thrown out of the town by the authorities.

The same things happened in Iconium – many were saved through Paul's preaching in the synagogue. Even though the authorities were against them, Paul and Barnabas stayed for a long time, and miracles were done through them.

But eventually, their enemies plotted to stone them, and so the apostles left. They turned up in Lystra, where a lame man was healed. The people tried to offer sacrifices to the apostles, because they were convinced that they were gods in human form. Paul and Barnabas denied this, but the people would not listen.

The people were stirred up by some Jews who came in from towns Paul had been in just before, and Paul was stoned and left for dead. But when the believers gathered round (presumably praying for him to be raised from the dead), he recovered and went off.

Acts 13:1–15:35

Amazingly, Paul and Barnabas travelled back the way they had come, through all the towns where they had met opposition, as well as seeing some saved.

When they got home, they told the Christians there what had happened.

Some people began to teach that you cannot be a Christian unless you are circumcised. Paul and Barnabas opposed this wrong teaching, and after many strong discussions, they went to Jerusalem to see the other apostles about it. They explained that Gentiles had been converted, but some Christians still said, "They must be circumcised."

Acts 13:1–15:35

The elders met to discuss the matter. Peter stood up and preached a short sermon on the grace of God.

Paul spoke about all the Gentiles who had been saved. James (the brother of Jesus) then suggested that they should inform the Gentiles that since God has given them salvation, they are saved. But it would be great if they obeyed three simple rules: avoid food sacrificed to idols; don't eat any animal that has been strangled, or any blood; and stay away from sexual immorality.

These guidelines were put in written form and Paul, Barnabas, Judas Barsabbas and Silas took the message back to the Christians in Antioch. Paul and Barnabas spent some time there.

Part Seven
(Acts 15:36–18:28)
A Change of Teams, a Change of Heart and a Change of Haircut

Paul and Barnabas wanted to go back through all the towns they had visited on their last journey, and Barnabas said, "Hey, let's take John Mark with us." He was the young man who had gone home shortly after the start of the last journey. Paul strongly disagreed and in the end they decided that Barnabas and Mark should go back to those churches, while Paul took Silas with him to Asia.

Paul met a man named Timothy in one of the towns he visited, and encouraged him to come with him and Silas.

The Holy Spirit didn't let them preach in some places they went to, and when they were on the border of Macedonia, Paul had a dream in the night about a man from Macedonia saying, "Come on over and help us!"

Luke, who must have been staying there, went with them. In Philippi, Paul, Silas, Timothy and Luke stayed with a woman named Lydia.

One day they were all going to a place of prayer when a clairvoyant woman followed them, shouting, "These men are servants of God! They announce to you how you can be saved!"

After this had gone on for a few days, Paul had had more than enough and spoke to the evil spirit that gave her the power to see into the future. "In the name of Jesus Christ I order you to come out of her!" She was immediately set free.

Acts of God

Trouble followed. The people who used to make money through her demonic powers seized Paul and Silas and dragged them to the authorities.

They ordered the apostles to be publicly whipped and beaten and then thrown into jail.

At midnight, the apostles were singing hymns when there was a massive earthquake, and the doors of the prison flew open with what can only be described as a great clang.

Acts 15:36–18:28

The jailer thought everyone had legged it and was about to do himself in with his sword when Paul stopped him. "Don't harm yourself! We are all here!"

The jailer realised that these were holy men, and after some conversation, he became a Christian, along with all his family. He washed the wounds of the apostles, and all the new Christians were baptised.

Next morning the official word came that Paul and Silas should be set free. But Paul made a fuss, because he had been publicly beaten, and now they wanted to send them away in private. "Not likely!", he said.

Paul was a Roman citizen, a status which gave people certain rights. The authorities came and apologised to them, but still threw them out of the city.

They left Luke in Philippi and went on to Thessalonica. They preached the gospel, but a mob was formed against them. Paul and Silas hid in the home of one of the local Christians, and then managed to escape.

They went to Berea, where the people received Paul and Silas more reasonably; they looked in the Old Testament to make sure he was telling the truth about God's Messiah.

Acts of God

Acts 15:36–18:28

But soon some Jews from Thessalonica came in and stirred up another mob. The local Christians thought it would be best if Paul moved on to Athens.

There Paul was impressed by an altar inscribed "To An Unknown God", and he preached an amazing sermon about God being the maker of the earth and Jesus His Son. Some were saved.

Paul went on to Corinth, where he met Aquila and Priscilla, an Italian Jewish couple. He was a tentmaker, like Paul, and they got on well together.

A while later, Silas and Timothy arrived, and Paul preached the good news. When they were again opposed by Jews, Paul told them he was now going to work with Gentiles.

God spoke to Paul in a vision, and said, "Keep on speaking fearlessly." Paul stayed there for eighteen months.

Some Jews seized Paul in the end, and tried to get him in trouble with the Roman authorities, but the local governor threw them all out of his chambers.

Later on, Paul took a vow and then had a skinhead cut, and went off with Aquila and Priscilla.

They went on to Ephesus, where the Italians stayed, and Paul went on to Antioch. Meanwhile, a Jew

Acts of God

named Apollos teamed up with the Italians and learned as much as they could teach him about the Lord. He then went off to spread the word elsewhere.

Part Eight
(Acts 19:1–21:32)
Trouble in Ephesus, and Big Trouble in Jerusalem

Paul, who had been travelling, found himself in Ephesus. He asked the disciples whether they were baptised in the Spirit or not.

They had never even heard of the Holy Spirit. So he baptised them in the name of Jesus, and they received the baptism of the Spirit.

For three months Paul spoke boldly in the synagogue, but when some refused to believe in Jesus he went off to another meeting place and stayed there for two years.

God was performing unusual miracles through Paul. Even handkerchiefs he had touched were taken to the sick and they recovered.

Seven Jewish brothers were commanding evil spirits to come out of people "in the name of Jesus whom

Acts of God

Paul preaches". One man who had an evil spirit cried out, "I know Jesus and I know about Paul, but who on earth are you?" Then he attacked them with great force, and they all ran away wounded and with their clothes torn.

Everyone in the town heard about this, and many repented of their magic, burning their expensive books of spells and potions.

Paul sent Timothy and a man named Erastus to Macedonia, and was thinking of going to Rome himself, but stayed on a little longer.

But about this time, one man who made statues of Diana, a goddess (also known as Artemis), got together with all the other silversmiths and convinced them that the Christians were bad for business. He explained that people were becoming followers of Jesus Christ and not buying the idols any more.

So they formed a mob and created a great riot.

This went on for more than two hours with all the people chanting, "Great is Diana of the Ephesians!" and "Great is Artemis of Ephesus!"

Paul left the town and spent three months in Achaia, where he met up again with Luke. They went on eventually to Troas.

Acts 19:1–21:32

Paul was preaching a sermon in a room on the third floor of a house one night and going on a bit. People were crowding in, and some were sitting on the windowsills. At about midnight, one young man dozed off and fell out of the window, and died. Paul went down and God raised the young man from the dead. Paul went back upstairs for a communion service and six more hours of sermon!

Paul was in a hurry to get to Jerusalem in time for Pentecost, and he called the elders of Ephesus Community Church for a final goodbye meeting. He spoke to them with great passion.

Paul and Luke went off and arrived at Tyre Christian Fellowship, where the believers urged Paul to avoid going to Jerusalem.

Acts 19:1–21:32

Nevertheless, Luke and Paul then went to Caesarea, and stayed with Philip, the man who had been chosen as one of the seven servants in Part Three. A prophet declared to them that Paul would be captured in Jerusalem, and handed over to the Gentiles. This did not put Paul off going, since he was willing to suffer (and even to die) for the sake of the gospel. He was convinced that he should go to Jerusalem, since the Holy Spirit had instructed him to do this.

When they got to Jerusalem, the church there had a brilliant meeting and Paul agreed to take part in a ceremony of purification. But at the end of the ceremony, Paul was seized by some Asian Jews and thrown out of the Temple. The mob tried to kill Paul, and...

Part Nine
(Acts 21:33–26:32)
Paul Gives Three Sermons, Survives Two Plots and Wins One Trip to Rome

...the Temple guards saved him and carried him over to the steps by the gate. Paul asked to speak to the Roman centurion, who gave him permission.

Paul, who was always keen to preach, then stood on the steps and preached an amazing sermon to everyone there. He told them how he was saved, and what God had done through him thus far.

The people interrupted after quite a while and the Romans were about to whip him when he quietly told them he was a Roman citizen. It would have been wrong of them to publicly whip a Roman citizen. So Paul was taken before the Jerusalem Council.

He told them, "My conscience is perfectly clear about the way in which I have lived to this very day."

Acts 21:33–26:32

The High Priest ordered the men standing by him to strike Paul on the mouth. Paul told him, "God will certainly strike you, you hypocrite!"

Paul knew the law about punishing a man while he was still on trial. When Paul found out that it was the High Priest, he didn't apologise but made it clear that he had not meant to break the rule about honouring the rulers.

Paul managed to cause a squabble among the Jews – some of them did believe in the resurrection of the dead, and others didn't.

Acts of God

While they were arguing with each other, the Romans thought Paul might be attacked, so they took him away to the fort. That night, the Lord encouraged Paul.

More than forty Jews got together the next morning and promised that they would not eat or drink again until they had killed Paul. But Paul's nephew heard about the plot and told Paul, who eventually got a message to the Roman commander.

The commander sent Paul off with 200 soldiers to the governor, whose name was Felix. He sent a letter explaining all the circumstances, and when Felix received the letter, he put Paul in prison to wait until those who were accusing him arrived.

It took them the best part of a week to get their act together, and they accused Paul of stirring up trouble, being a dangerous nuisance and attempting to defile the Temple.

Paul then got a chance to speak, and guess what? He preached an amazing sermon, and Felix, who knew quite a lot about Christians, listened with interest.

Paul was kept under house arrest in Felix's palace for two years, until Felix was succeeded by another Roman, who gloried in the marvellous name of Porcius Festus.

Jews begged Festus to send Paul back to Jerusalem, so that they could kill him on the way. Festus answered, "No way, José," even though he wanted to be popular. He asked Paul if he would be willing to go to Jerusalem to be tried.

Paul officially asked for his case to be tried by the Emperor, Caesar, in Rome. Festus had little choice but to promise to send him to Rome.

A while later, King Agrippa heard about the case, and after discussing it with Festus, he wanted to hear Paul speak. So Paul was brought in, and he – you guessed it – preached an amazing sermon, including the story of how he was converted, and of the work he had done by God's miraculous power.

Eventually, the Italian governor Festus interrupted him with a shout. "You-a crazy man! You-a out-a your mind! You-a need-a your head examined!"

"I am not insane, your excellency," Paul replied. "I am speaking the truth."

The King was impressed, and said, "If only he had not appealed to be tried by Caesar – I have the power to release him." But Paul wanted to go to Rome, which he does in our final episode.

Part Ten
(Acts 27:1–28:31)
A Storm, a Sandbank, a Shipwreck and a Snake

Luke and Paul are handed over to Julius, a Roman officer, and they set sail. Julius let Paul see some friends when they stopped on the way, and they later joined another ship that was going to Rome.

Due to unfavourable October winds, they were blown off course and ended up near a place called Safe Harbours.

While the sailors were keen to keep going, because they would have hated staying in such a place as Safe Harbours for any time, Paul could see it was impossible to make any more headway.

But the captain of the ship went on.

Disaster struck, as a huge gale blew the little ship miles off course. They found somewhere relatively safe, throwing cargo overboard to lighten the load.

Acts of God

Acts 27:1–28:31

Luke gave up all hope of being saved from the gale, so great was the storm.

Paul said to everyone, "I told you so. We could have avoided all this. But listen. Last night an angel told me that not one of you would be lost. We will be driven ashore on an island."

After a fortnight at sea, the sailors tried to get away on a lifeboat, because they were afraid the ship would be driven onto rocks and break up.

But Paul said, "No one will survive if the crew desert us now!" So the Romans cut the lifeboat off before the sailors could get into it.

The next morning, the ship hit a sandbank and ran aground – the ship was broken to pieces by the force of the hurricane.

The soldiers were about to kill all the prisoners, to prevent them from swimming ashore and escaping.

But the officer wanted to save Paul, so he stopped them.

He ordered all the men who could swim to go ashore, and the rest followed on, holding onto driftwood from the smashed ship.

Everyone was saved, as the angel had promised.

Acts of God

They landed on Malta and Paul was about to build a fire when a snake crawled out of the heap of sticks he was holding.

The people saw Paul being bitten by the snake, and then he shook it off into the fire.

Everyone waited for him to swell up or fall down dead as a dodo, but when it didn't happen, they assumed, "He is a god!"

The chief of the island asked them all to stay with him.

Paul prayed for his father, who was suffering from an infection which resulted in a high temperature and various other reactions, some of which resulted in unpleasantness. He recovered, and all the people brought their sick to Paul and they were healed by the mighty power of God.

Three months later they set sail again, and after a long journey Luke and Paul arrived in Rome.

The members of the King's Church, Rome, came to visit, as well as other believers from other towns nearby.

Paul was allowed to live by himself, as long as a soldier was on guard all the time. Paul called the local Jewish leaders to a meeting, where he told them

Acts 27:1–28:31

about his trials, imprisonments and adventures. Then he preached an amazing sermon about the inheritance they have as Jews, and the importance of believing in Jesus Christ.

Some believed, but many disputed various technical prophecies in the Old Testament. Paul's comment: "The message of salvation has been sent to Gentiles. They will listen!"

For two years more Paul lived in Rome, and preached with great boldness.

Glossary

page 11 **apostles.** Literally, the word means "one who is sent" but in the New Testament it tends to indicate those appointed and anointed by God to plant churches and have a serious ministry of evangelism and discipleship.

page 12 **Pentecost.** A Jewish day of feasting and celebration – literally fifty days after Passover.

page 12 **filled with the Holy Spirit.** Jesus promised that when He ascended to His Father, He would send a Helper, a Counsellor, a Guide to His disciples. The Holy Spirit enables Christians to be bold, gives spiritual gifts and confirms that we belong to God if we have confessed our sin and put our faith in the Lord Jesus Christ. If you want to know more, you might like Malcolm Kyte's *Catch the Wind* if you're a younger reader, or Phil Rogers and Terry Virgo's *Receiving the Holy Spirit and His Gifts* for older readers.

page 12 **repent.** To turn round completely. To go in the opposite direction. This is what you do if you want to give up following sin and the way of destruction, and turn round to God, confess your sin and become a Christian.

page 13 **miracles.** Literally, a miracle is something that cannot happen. We sometimes refer to the laws of nature – for example, gravity. But really those laws are just a way of explaining what normally happens, and since God is supernatural, He can choose to make a miracle – something extraordinary – happen. The dead are raised to life, a lame man is made whole, the blind see, and people who are dead in sin can become alive in Christ.

page 14 **Temple.** The large building in Jerusalem set aside for the worship of God. The physically afflicted were placed at the gates by their family or by those who took pity on them so that they could beg from people going in and out of the Temple.

page 15 **boldness.** This is not the same as fearlessness, but means that you do what you're scared about anyway. In the disciples' case, boldness was something God gave them as they got on with the job. They were not like Rambo or someone who stupidly continues without fear, but like you and me. They were probably scared to death, but relied on God's power and greatness to help them get through. Please note that sometimes their boldness resulted in them being whipped and imprisoned. What do you do for God? Hmm?

page 16 **whip.** Getting a beating from a Roman soldier was a serious punishment. The whip did not just sting your skin – it was often a cat-o'-nine-tails, with bits of metal and flint tied into the thongs of leather, efficiently designed to tear flesh from your back.

page 24 **Gentile.** A non-Jew. Jews were taught from an early age that since Jews were God's chosen race, Gentiles

Glossary

were different and didn't enjoy God's blessing. It was hard for Jews to accept that God was allowing Gentiles to become Christians, and baptising them in the Holy Spirit.

page 26 **King Herod.** This is not the King Herod who reigned in Palestine at the time of the birth of Jesus – he died in 4 BC (yes, they got the dating of the nativity slightly wrong). This was Herod II.

page 28 **synagogue.** The local place of worship for Jews. The apostles often preached in synagogues since visitors were invited to do so. It made sense, because the apostles wanted to spread the good news to the Jews as well as to the Gentiles.

page 30 **sacrifices.** It would have been quite wrong for the apostles to have allowed the people to have worshipped them in this way, since they were men empowered by God, not gods themselves.

page 32 **circumcision.** A ritual best performed on newborn babies; a physical symbol of Jewishness (for men). See Exodus 4:25.

page 33 **sexual immorality.** It was part of the local culture in those days for people to indulge in orgies and other wild parties. The guidelines made it clear that such behaviour was unacceptable for those who were now born again.

page 33 **the guidelines.** Why did these guidelines have to be set up? God knew that Jews found it difficult to

Acts of God

accept Gentiles as Christian brothers and sisters after centuries of distinction. None of these guidelines were bad rules – meat sacrificed to idols and sexual immorality are both things to avoid. Some Christians feel that the laws about animals that had been strangled, and about blood were included to allow the Hebrew Christians some time to adjust from their Jewish way of life to the freedom found in Christianity.

page 35 **clairvoyant.** Someone who sees, or claims to see, into the future. When God empowers someone to declare what will happen in the future, this is one form of prophecy. When credit is not given to God, the person who spoke must have either been making it up himself, or have been empowered by Satan.

page 37 **Roman citizen.** In those days, a person could buy Roman citizenship, which gave them certain privileges – including the right to be tried before Caesar, and the right to be treated with dignity and respect.

page 39 **vow.** A serious promise before God. Obviously, this promise involved the use of a cheap barber.

page 41 **handkerchiefs.** I am led to believe that people brought clean handkerchiefs to Paul for him to pray over, which they then took back to their sick friends. It might have been somewhat unhygienic if they had carried Paul's crusty old handkerchief around.

The Storyline Series

Dan the Man
by Andy Back

Daniel and his three friends remain obedient to the Lord as they face trials and trouble in a foreign land! A story of sand, lions, fires, idols, kings, madness, faith, visions, vegetables, graffiti and godliness.

Be like Daniel! Feel the hot breath of the lions against the back of your neck! Trust God to help you as the King makes extraordinary and unreasonable demands! Be amazed and excited at what God is doing as you face strange and bewildering beasts!

The drama of the book of Daniel unfolds in modern language, making these true stories as fresh as the day they were written.

Dan the Man is another exciting title in this series. 64 pp. Illustrated throughout.

Published by
Word (UK) Ltd./Frontier Publishing International